KILLER FLOOD

JEFF GOTTESFELD

SADDLEBACK
EDUCATIONAL PUBLISHING

red rhino
b OO k s™

With more titles on the way …

SADDLEBACK
EDUCATIONAL PUBLISHING
www.sdlback.com

ISBN-13: 978-1-62250-946-1
ISBN-10: 1-62250-946-3
eBook: 978-1-63078-170-5

Printed in Guangzhou, China
NOR/1014/CA21401612

19 18 17 16 15   1 2 3 4 5

Dan

Age: 12

Fun Fact: holds the school record for most cell phones lost or destroyed

Future Goal: to be an airline pilot

Biggest Fish Caught: seven-pound largemouth bass

Best Quality: calm under pressure

Homer

Age: 92

Favorite Breakfast: two poached eggs on toast with maple-flavored sausage on the side

Unusual Hobby: collects old lightbulbs

Can't Eat This Anymore: 3 Musketeers

Best Quality: great sense of humor

1
BIG RAIN

Dan looked out the window. It was night. Outside was pitch black. The sound of rain was loud.

"Still coming down," he reported.

Dan's best friend, Pete, rolled his eyes. "It's been raining for a week. I'm sick of being inside. No baseball. And more rain is coming."

They were next door at the Lands' house. Old Mr. Land laughed. "I don't need you to tell me. My hands ache. They always ache when it rains."

His wife made a funny face. "Homer, your hands ache no matter."

Mr. Land grinned. "My dear wife. I'm ninety-two years old. They're supposed to ache."

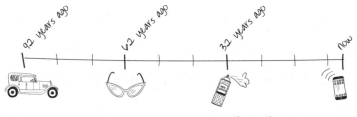

century (100 yrs) TIMELINE

"Just take your medicines, Mister Land," Dan reminded him.

Mr. Land was a great guy. Dan loved him and Ellie, his wife. He was as smart as a whip. He used to take Dan fishing at Fish Lake. They had a lot of luck near the big dam. Sometimes they would fish the river below the dam. Water from the lake fed the river.

Mr. Land was also a great darts player. But he had a lot of health stuff. The biggest issue was with his blood sugar. He had diabetes. He had to test his blood all the time. If the sugar level was bad, he had to inject medicine. Without the medicine, he could die.

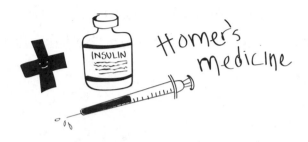

"Don't worry about me," Mr. Land told the boys. "I'm going to live to two hundred. Who wants to play darts?"

Dan checked the time on his cell. His parents and Pete's parents had gone to the city. They went for a show. They would be back very late.

They had told Dan and Pete to be in bed by ten. Pete was sleeping over. It was no big thing for the kids to stay alone. The town was very safe. Plus, the Lands lived next-door.

"One more game," Dan told Mr. Land.

"Good." Mr. Land turned to his wife. "Woman? Bring us some chips!"

Everyone laughed. Mr. Land loved to poke fun at his wife. But he really loved her. He needed her too. She took care of him.

Dan was also a good darts player. He was small for his age. But he had a great eye. Darts took skill, not power. He won easily.

They call Dan laser eye

After the game, Dan and Pete said good night. They ran back to Dan's house. When they got there, they played a few video games and fed the cat, Fluffy. Dan texted his folks.

"Back from Lands'. Cat fed. Going to bed. CU later."

There was no text back. Dan was sure they were still at the show. They would go out to eat too. It was a long trip to the city. In the rain, it would be longer. He would see them in the morning.

Dan lived in a one-story house. There were bunk beds in his room. He would get the top bunk. Pete would be below. He plugged in his cell and put it on a table. Just as Pete came out of the bathroom, Dan's cell sounded with an ugly tone. So did Pete's.

"What the heck?" Pete asked.

Dan checked his phone. "It's a warning. Flash flood."

"I got the same thing," Pete said.

"It's the river. Because of the rain," Dan

said. "It's happened before. No prob for us. I'm going to brush my teeth. Do not even think about putting sand in my bed."

"Sand? Sand? Are you kidding?" Pete hooted. "In this rain? It's mud!"

FLOOD

WARNING!

2
STRANGE SOUNDS

Dan brushed his teeth and washed his face. Then he went back to his bedroom. Pete was already under the covers on the bottom bunk. Dan climbed to the top.

"Turn out the light, dude," he told his friend.

Pete turned out the light. They could hear the rain on the roof. If anything, it was coming down harder.

Pete's eyes in the dark

"You remember the last flash flood?" Pete asked.

"Two years ago, right?"

"Yep. They closed Main Street for a day. The ball field was underwater for a week," Pete recalled. "The town is so low. That's the problem. Water just pools up."

"Maybe you need to quit baseball. Take up swimming," Dan told him.

"You know I can't swim—"

"Shush!" Dan told his friend suddenly. He had heard something. Something strange.

Like water running in the bathroom. "You hear that?"

"The water?" Pete asked. "You forgot to turn it off?"

Dan slid down to the floor. "I've got it. I can't believe it. I never forget to turn off the water."

"You are up too late. That's why."

Dan flipped on the light and turned to his friend. "Pete?"

"Yeah?"

"Shut up. I'll be right back."

As he stepped down the hall to the bathroom, the gurgle was louder. Strange.

It didn't sound like it was coming from the sink.

"You hear that?" he called to Pete.

"Hear what? The rain? Yeah. It blows."

Dan stopped at the bathroom. The water was off. But the strange sound was still there. He followed it to the living room. He turned on the light.

"Uh-oh!"

He stopped dead. Water was gushing into the house. It came in around the front door. More came from the kitchen. Some came from the outlets. It was already a few inches deep on the floor.

Pete called from the bedroom. "Hey! The floor is wet!"

Dan yelled back. "Pete! Get your butt out here! Now!"

3
BLACKOUT

The water rose quickly. It was three feet high in five minutes. Dan and Pete got on the dining room table. They were safe there. At least for a little while.

My rubber ducky

"Where's your cell?" Dan asked Pete.
Pete frowned. "I left it on the floor. In

your room. It must underwater. Dang it. What about yours?"

"I think it's still on the table. Let me go see."

Dan jumped off the table. The water came to his waist. Whoa. It was deep. And cold. And the color of dirt. At least the lights were still on. He waded slowly to the bedroom.

Yes! There it was. His phone was still on the nightstand. He grabbed it. Called 911. He heard a strange beeping sound. He tried again. Same thing. He tried his parents. Same thing.

He called to Pete. "Got the phone! But no service!" Then he waded back to Pete. He held his cell high so it would not get wet. Pete helped him back up.

"How much juice you got?" Pete asked.

Dan shivered. He was wet and cold. He looked at his cell. "Some. Not much." He was able to connect to the Internet. He went to a news page. The alert was on the home screen.

"Warning!" he read to Pete. *"Fish Lake Dam Break! Green Valley Flooded! Town Cut Off!"*

Dan shook. This time it was not from cold. But from fear. The dam had burst. It had failed because of the all the rain. Water was pouring into town. Sure, it would flow out. But not for a long time.

He and Pete were trapped. With the town cut off, there would be no help for now.

Pete had read the alert too. "Man. This is bad, Dan. Try your folks again."

Dan did. No luck. No cell. No roads. No help. He and Pete were on their own.

Pete looked a little sick. "How high will the water come? Because I can't swim, you know."

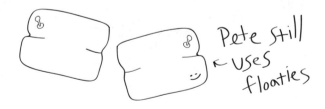

Pete still
← uses
floaties

"Dunno. And I don't want to wait to find out." Dan had a plan in his mind. "We need to get out of here. Get to a high place."

"High? We live in a valley. There is no high place here!"

Dan pointed to the front door. "Not inside. Outside. Like the roof. Or the tree house. The one near the road. In the ash tree."

Pete nodded. "Yeah. I remember the tree house. We haven't been in it for a long time."

Built 5 summers ago

"It's about to save our lives. Let's go."

They climbed down off the table and into the cold water. It now came to Dan's chest. Pete was a little taller. They started to wade. Dan held his cell high. If it got wet, it would be ruined. At some point, maybe there would be service again. Then they could call for help.

They were halfway to the door when the power failed.

The lights went out. They were stuck in the rising water. They could not see their hands in front of their faces. It was not just dark. It was black.

4
DUMB MOVE

Dan had known dark and wet before. But not like this. Not with icy water up to his chest. Not when he did not know where he was.

He was afraid to turn for fear of losing his bearings. He did not know where his eyes ended and the dark started.

"Oh my gosh. Oh my gosh. Oh my gosh," Pete repeated. "I can't see. I can't see anything!"

← Complete darkness

"Quiet," Dan ordered. He had to think. He could not do that with Pete so upset.

Pete didn't listen. "What do we do now?"

"We get out of this. But we have to stay calm. And think. So be quiet!"

Pete was his best bud. Dan did not like to yell at him. But Pete was not helping. In fact, he was hurting them.

What to do?

Dan had his cell phone. He held it high. Above the water. If he got it wet, it would go dead. He could not get it wet. But if he touched the right button …

The screen lit up. It put out a blue light.

Glows

"Your phone!" Pete exclaimed. "I can see a little now."

"And if I find the right app ..." Dan brought his cell as close to his face as he dared. He did not want it near the water. He changed screens. Somewhere, he had an app ...

He had it!

Pete

The flashlight app. A beam of light cut the darkness. He pointed it at Pete. His friend was white with fear. His eyes were big. His hands shook. Dan knew he had to be the leader.

"Okay. Back to the table," he told Pete. "Then we'll figure this out."

Dan trained the beam on the dining room table. They could not stay there long. But they could rest a moment. Pete sloshed over to it. Dan followed. This was the right thing to—

"Nooo! Dang it!"

Dan fell forward. He had stepped on something. It had slid under his foot. He started to fall. Down went his hands to break the fall. The cell in his hand plunged into the water. The moment it hit the water, it failed. The room went black again.

Slipped on this →

Statue of our cat, Fluffy ←

"No, no, no! I am such a klutz!" he shouted. "What a dumb move."

"What happened?" Pete called. "Turn your phone back on!"

"Can't. I soaked it. Keep talking. I'll come to you."

There was nothing more he could do. Pete called. Dan followed the sound. He got to the table. He boosted himself up. He found he was still holding the cell phone. Angry at himself, he threw it into the water.

"What do we do now?" Pete asked. His question was followed by far off thunder.

Dan waited until the thunder was over before he answered. Not that it was a good answer.

"Pete? I don't have a clue."

5
FLUFFY

Dan took a deep breath. There were so many things going wrong. They were soaked. The water was cold. They had not eaten a real meal in a long time. If they lost too much body heat, they could die. It was too dark to see. Dan did not even know where the door was.

A flash of lightning lit the room. It was followed by a roll of thunder.

The lightning was what Dan needed. He got his bearings. The front door was a bit to the left. He and Pete could get to it. Then they could get outside. Then get to the tree house. But what about the lightning?

Lightning ♥s trees

The worst place to be in a storm was in a tree. Or near a tree. At least it was one tree among many. They would be above the rising water. Better to fry by lightning than to drown.

More lightning. Dan saw the door again.

"Okay. We're going to the tree house," he told Pete. "Let's just—"

Meow.

They both heard it.

Meow, meow, meow!

Fluffy the cat was crying. Dan wondered if she had been crying the whole time. Had they missed it? Or had she just started? Was she crying because she was wet? Where was she anyway?

"You hear that?" Pete asked.

"I'm not deaf," Dan said.

"Ignore it," Pete told him. "She'll be fine. Let's go outside."

Dan shook his head. He loved that cat.

He was not going to let her die. "Nope. We need to check on her."

"Are you crazy?" Pete asked. "She's just a cat. She'll be fine. Let's go—"

Dan didn't like what Pete said. He cared about the cat. He had to be sure she was okay. The cries came from the kitchen. A flash of lightning lit the way to the kitchen door.

Dan jumped off the table. "I'm getting her. Come if you want."

He waded. The water was still rising. The splashes behind him said Pete was following. He went many feet into the darkness.

He banged the wall with his face. It hurt. A lot.

Where was the door? Where was it?

Lightning showed him it was to his right. He felt his way there, foot by foot. Then he was inside. Fluffy meowed again.

"I'm coming, Fluffy!" he called.

More meows.

Now he was in the kitchen. A bolt of lightning showed him where the cat was. She was on top of the fridge. Safely out of danger. It would take a flood like in the Bible to reach her. The cat was safe. Well, wasn't that what they said? Cats always land on—

The thought hit him like a fist. The moment he thought "land."

The cat was safe. He would be okay on the fridge for now. But there were others who might not be safe. The people next-door. The people so old they could not help themselves.

The Lands.

6
HELP US! PLEASE!

The Lands' house

Dan and Pete reached the Lands' house. It had been so hard to get there. They had to wade. The water was deep. The footing was rough. Rain was still pouring down. Lightning flashed. Thunder rolled. Pete held Dan's arm all the way. He was so afraid of falling since he couldn't swim.

Dan had another fear. He knew science. Water guides electricity. They were up to their chests in water. If lightning hit the water, it would shoot through like a live wire. He and Pete were in the middle of that live wire. They would be fried. They would die. The only good part was they would feel only one shock.

"Gotta hurry. Gotta hurry," he kept saying.

"I am hurrying!" Pete told him.

They sloshed up the walk to Lands' front

door. The water was heavy. It took two of them to push the door open.

Phew! They were inside.

Dan knew the house well. It was on two levels. On the first level were the living room, dining room, and kitchen. Upstairs were two bedrooms. One was for the Lands. The other was for guests. There was a faint glow of light from upstairs. That was good. Light meant life.

Glow from upstairs

"Hello? Hello?" he called. "Mister Land? Mrs. Land? You guys okay?"

There was no answer.

"Hello?" Pete yelled.

Still no answer. That was bad. The Lands may have been in the living room when the water came. Maybe they were watching TV. Or reading on the couch. The water may have been too deep.

What if Mr. Land fell? And Mrs. Land tried to help him. But Mr. Land was so big. Maybe she hurt her back. Or her leg. Or something. Maybe Mr. Land drowned. Maybe they drowned.

Maybe there were two dead bodies! He was freaking out now.

Dan stepped on something. It squished under his foot.

A body!

He was about to scream in horror. Then he realized it was just a pillow.

36

Just a ← pillow

"They're not answering," Pete said.

"You are not being helpful, Pete," Dan said. He felt sick. But there was still the light. Dan pointed to the stairs. Water covered the lower steps. "Let's check it out."

They waded over and started up. On the landing there was a flashlight. That was a good sign. It meant someone had put it there. It could mean the Lands were here. But where were they? Why didn't they respond?

"Hello?" Dan bellowed. "Anyone here? Mister Land? Mrs. Land? Hello?"

This time, there was an answer. It came from one of the bedrooms.

"Help!" The voice was female. But it was weak. "Help us! Help us, please!"

7
LIFE OR DEATH

The boys were with Mrs. Land a few seconds later. The Lands were in the main bedroom. A few candles burned. Mr. Land was on the bed.

Mrs. Land told the story. They had been in the living room. Then the flood came. She took Mr. Land upstairs. She forgot his medicine. It was on the coffee table. Also his test kits. Mr. Land needed them. If he did not get them, he could die.

"We can find them," Pete told her. "I don't swim. But I can feel around on the floor."

Dan shook his head. "It's no good. They won't be clean. We have to get all new stuff."

"Right," Pete jeered. "In this storm. In this flood. Good luck."

"I know. We need a drugstore," Dan said.

"The closest one is downtown. On Main Street."

Dan nodded. "Yep. We need to go there."

"Downtown?" Pete shouted. "Are you nuts? Downtown must be underwater too!"

"I don't think that's a good idea," Mrs. Land told Dan.

Dan looked over at Mr. Land. His old friend was facedown. He moaned. Dan knew he was in bad shape.

"Mrs. Land? It's the best idea we've got." He put a hand on Mrs. Land's arm. It felt dry. Almost like paper. She was in better shape than Mr. Land. But she was old too. He had to help them. He just had to. "Write down what we need. We can break into the store if we have to."

Dan wants to do this!

"That's a crime. We can go to jail!" Pete got upset again.

"We have to do this," he told Pete. He

turned to Mrs. Land. "We'll be back." He looked at his bud. "Pete? You coming or not?"

"Yeah." Pete nodded. "I'm in."

"At least put on dry clothes," Mrs. Land insisted. "You boys are in your pj's."

The Lands had some kids' clothes in the guest room. Mrs. Land found them dry things. The boys changed. It would all get soaked. But it was good to be dry. Even for a minute.

Mrs. Land made a list. She put it in a baggie for Dan. She gave him a flashlight. Then they said good-bye.

Dan led Pete down to the living room. The water was high. So much for dry clothes.

"What's our plan?" Pete asked.

"Follow me."

Dan knew where Mr. Land kept his fishing boat. It was tied up behind the garage. It would be full of rainwater. If it was even there. He and Pete would need to dump the water. At least Dan knew how to drive it.

The boys waded behind the garage. Yes! There was the boat. It was bobbing in the water.

"Boost me up," Dan told Pete.

What's that doing there??

Pete helped Dan in. The key was in it. Also some buckets. Dan turned the key to start the motor. Nothing. He tried again. Nothing.

"Bad, dude," Pete said.

"Get in," Dan told him. "Use the buckets. Bail the water."

"But the engine!"

"Pete? Make yourself useful. Scoop the water out!" Dan reached under the seat. There were two paddles. Just in case the engine died on the lake. He held them up. Sighed. "We'll row."

Five minutes later, each boy had an oar.

It was a mile to downtown. They started to row. Dan had no idea what they would find. Main Street would be underwater. It would take luck to get into the drugstore. And it had not been a lucky night so far.

At least they were rowing with the current. And it had stopped raining.

8
HANDS UP!

Dan's back hurt. His hands hurt. He had blisters. So did Pete. But they rowed to Main Street. On the way, they saw awful things. Animals in the water. Houses on fire. Cars on their sides. Downed power lines.

The one good thing was hearing the distant sirens. Maybe help was coming. It took a long time to get to Main Street. When Dan felt weak, he remembered sick Mr. Land. They had to hurry.

Finally, they got close to downtown. There were fire trucks there. Firefighters and police officers stood on the trucks.

Dan got to his feet. He shined his light on a truck. Then he called out. "Hey! Hey!" he screamed.

A man yelled back into the darkness. "Who's out there?"

Dan could not see his face. But he saw lights cut into the night. Then, one was on him and Pete.

"Police! Put up your hands! Hands up! Both of you!" the cop ordered.

Blisters from rowing

"Don't shoot!" Dan yelled back. He put

his hands in the air. So did Pete. "I'm Dan. This is Pete. We're just kids! We need help!"

This was met with silence. The light was still in his face. His heart pounded. He hoped the police officer was not trigger-happy.

"Okay! Here's what I want." The cop was in charge. "The kid sitting. You row. The other? Stay on your feet!"

Pete found the oars. He rowed the boat toward the fire truck.

Dan grabbed the truck's side.

misses his family

(A. GLASS)

The cop was mad. "Why are you kids out?

You think this is fun? You think this is a joke? You want to get hurt? Go home!"

Dan tried to explain. "We are not out for fun. We need help."

The cop got angrier. "Kid, everyone needs help. Just wait your turn."

"Why don't you listen?" Dan yelled. It was wrong to scream at a cop. But he had to make the guy understand. "There's an old man. He lives next-door. He's sick. He can't get his medicine. He needs more. Or he'll die. We'll take it back to him."

Dan dug into his pocket. He took out Mrs. Land's list. It was still in the baggie. "His wife gave me this. Look!"

Went from this ⟶ To this

The cop shined his light on the paper. His eyes got big. "How far did you kids row?"

It felt like forever. But it didn't matter how far. They were here now. "A mile. Maybe. Please. Get us in the drugstore?"

The cop moved closer. "A lot of folks will die tonight. This is a killer flood. But maybe we can save a life. Come on."

9
MAIN STREET

The police officer's name was Glass. The boys made room for him in the boat. He had a superstrong flashlight. Dan pointed it down the street. Officer Glass rowed strong. Very soon, they were in the middle of Main Street.

Dan looked around in horror. What a mess. The clothes store. The food store. The auto parts store. The diner. The sporting goods store. All had broken windows. The force of the flood had been too strong. Water filled the shops.

There were odd bubbles in the road. Dan figured out those bubbles were the tops of cars. What had happened to the people in those cars?

The drugstore was at the end of the street. They got closer.

"Where are your folks, kids?" Officer Glass asked.

Pete answered. "In the city. They went to a show."

"Give me their numbers. I'll get word to them that you're okay."

"You can call them?" Dan was so happy.

"Nah. I'll tell my boss on the radio. He'll take care of it." Officer Glass pulled on the oars.

Over and out!

The boys told the cop the numbers. Then they got to the drugstore. The windows were busted. The store was flooded. Officer Glass rowed right into the store. Dan pointed the way.

"Drugs are in the back," the cop said. "I just hope ..."

"Hope what?" Dan asked.

The cop pulled hard on the oars. "Hope

this isn't all for nothing. Pray what we need is dry."

Dan gulped. He had not thought of that.

They got to the drug counter. Officer Glass took off his gun, his belt, and his radio. Then he jumped into the water.

"Shine the light for me," he told Dan.

"I want to help," Dan said.

The cop stopped. "That's against the rules." He seemed to think. "Well … okay. Pete, you take the light."

Dan jumped into the water. It was cold. He waded into the drug area. He knew what to look for. Blood test kits. Needles. And the meds for Mr. Land.

He and Officer Glass split up. Pete tried to shine the light for both of them. So many drugs were below water. They were ruined.

Dan had no luck. Neither did the cop.

"Okay," said Officer Glass. "We can give this about one more—"

Suddenly, Dan shouted. "I got it! I got it!"

It was right in front of him. An area marked Diabetes. The drugs. The needles. The test kits. They were all dry. He found a bag and filled it up. The police officer helped. Dan was so excited. Then he got more excited. He heard the sound of a motorboat.

Officer Glass was soaked, but he still

grinned. "That's our ride. Your ride, I should say. It'll take you where you're going."

"What about this boat?" Pete called.

"It's safe with me."

Dan watched as a police powerboat came right into the store. It pulled up next to Mr. Land's fishing boat. There were two rescue workers in it.

"These are the boys," Officer Glass told the workers. "I'll take their boat back to my station. Please take them where they need to go."

The rescue workers helped Dan and Pete into their boat. A minute later, they roared away. In a boat with power, they could be at the Lands' house fast. But was it already too late? Dan hoped not.

10
ONE YEAR LATER

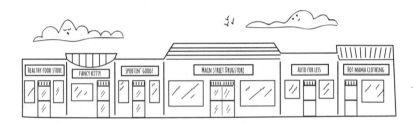

Everyone came to Main Street one year after the flood. All the water was gone. All the shops were open. Everything was clean. The dam was rebuilt. It was stronger than ever. There would be no more floods. One was bad enough. Too many people had died.

Chairs were set up on the street. Those who had helped save lives would be thanked. There would be speeches and music. Dan and Pete went with their parents. There were seats in front just for them.

So fancy

Mr. and Mrs. Land were already there. They were all dressed up. Mr. Land stood with his cane when Dan came near. He stuck out his hand.

"How's my lifesaver?" He turned to Dan's parents. "I've said it before. I'll say it again. And again. I owe your son my life."

Dan spoke up. "Pete too."

"Of course. Pete too."

Dan recalled the last part of that terrible night. The night of the killer flood. The rescue boat had sped them to the Lands'.

He and Pete took the meds inside. Mr. Land was close to death. Mrs. Land gave Mr. Land a shot. The medics took care of him. Mr. Land got better. It was the best moment of Dan's life.

The mayor gave a speech. He had a number of people stand so the crowd could see them. He praised the rescue workers. The fire fighters. The police officers. The two boys were last.

"They say kids are good for nothing." The mayor looked over the crowd. "That they only care about video games. Taking selfies.

Texting. I am here to say it is not true. You all know the story of Dan and Pete. These kids saved a life. They didn't have to. They faced danger. They put their own lives at risk. They can show us all how to be better people."

Then the mayor asked the boys to stand.

Dan did not feel like he had done anything so great. Mr. Land was his friend. His friend was sick. He'd helped. That was all.

Dan wanted Mr. Land to stand. So he and Pete helped him to his feet. They stood by him as the crowd clapped. The clapping went on for a long time. Finally, Dan smiled. It had been a killer flood. Dan had helped save a life.

The mayor was right. It was way better than video games.